THE PURPLE TURTLE

BY
TRADESHA WOODARD

ISBN: 979-888896920-5 (Paperback)
ISBN: 979-888895511-6 (Hardcover)

Published by Endless StoryHouse

Book Illustrations, Book Layout & eBook conversion by manuscript2ebook.com

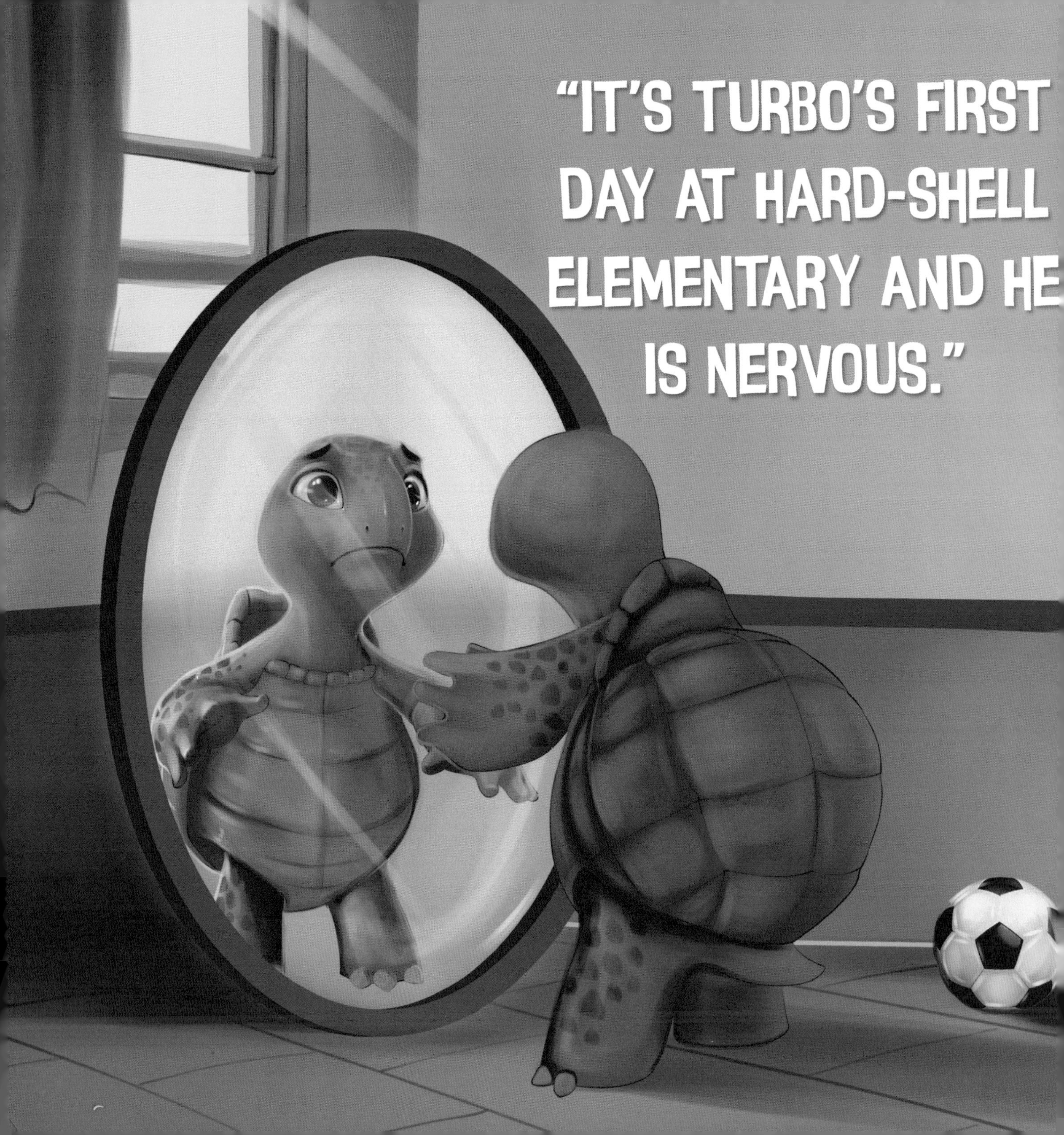
"IT'S TURBO'S FIRST DAY AT HARD-SHELL ELEMENTARY AND HE IS NERVOUS."

He is nervous as he eats his breakfast.
He is nervous as he packs his school bag.
He is nervous as his mom drives him to school.

"We are here Turbo," says Mom.
"Are you ready for your first day, Turbo?"
"What if I don't fit in?" asks Turbo.
"What if no one wants to be my friend?"
"Be brave," Mom says. "I'm sure you'll find
someone who wants to be friends with the
coolest turtle in town!"

Hard-Shell
Elementary School

Turbo cracks a smile. "I'll do my best, Mom." He climbs out of the car, waves goodbye, and walks towards the school.

As Turbo walks inside, he starts to tense up.
He slowly creeps down the hallway.
As he walks past other students, they turn and stare at him.
"Hi, I'm Turbo," he says quietly.
Hi, I'm Turbo.

For a moment, no one speaks.
Then someone says, “Ewww, why is he purple?”
Everyone suddenly starts laughing and pointing at
Turbo. Tears form in Turbo’s eyes. He turns and runs.
Ewww, why is he purple?

As Turbo speeds down the hall, he bumps into a teacher.
“Slow down,” says Mrs. Flippy. “You must be Turbo. Come on in and have a seat.”

Turbo walks in nervously. All the students stare at him.
Turbo sits in an empty seat near Mack.
"Eww," says Mack, moving his desk away. "No one wants to sit next to a PURPLE turtle!"
GROSS!

As the class starts to giggle, Turbo closes his eyes and buries his face in his desk.
“I just want to go home,” he mumbles.
I just want to go home.

When the bell rings for recess, the class heads outside to play.
There are so many fun things to do, and Turbo has no idea where to start.

Turbo decides to play with the football first, but Mack kicks the ball away.
Then Turbo reaches for the basketball, but Mack snatches it out of his hands.
“Don’t touch anything!” says Mack. “You might turn it purple!”

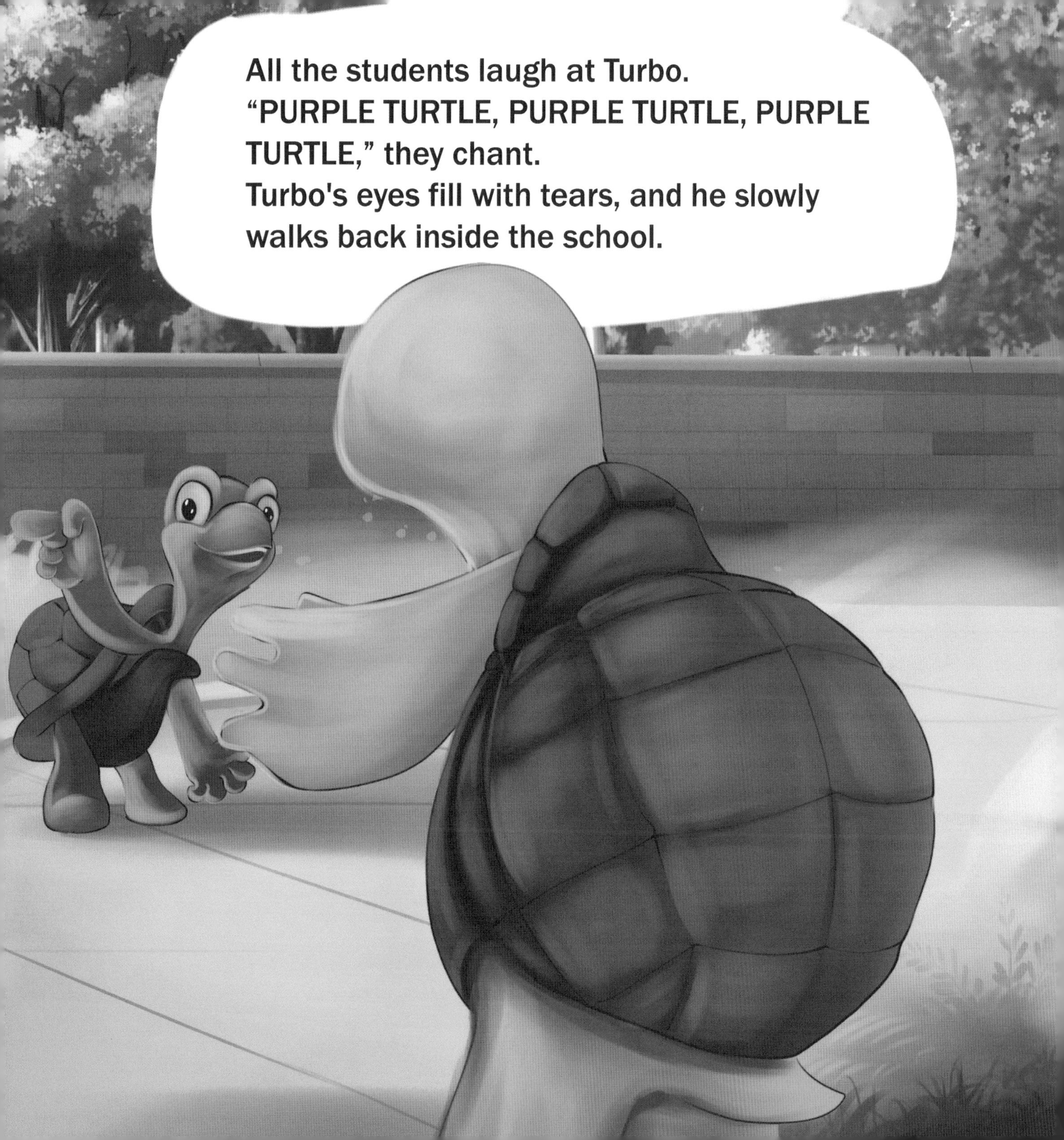

All the students laugh at Turbo.
"PURPLE TURTLE, PURPLE TURTLE, PURPLE TURTLE," they chant.
Turbo's eyes fill with tears, and he slowly walks back inside the school.

Why am I purple?

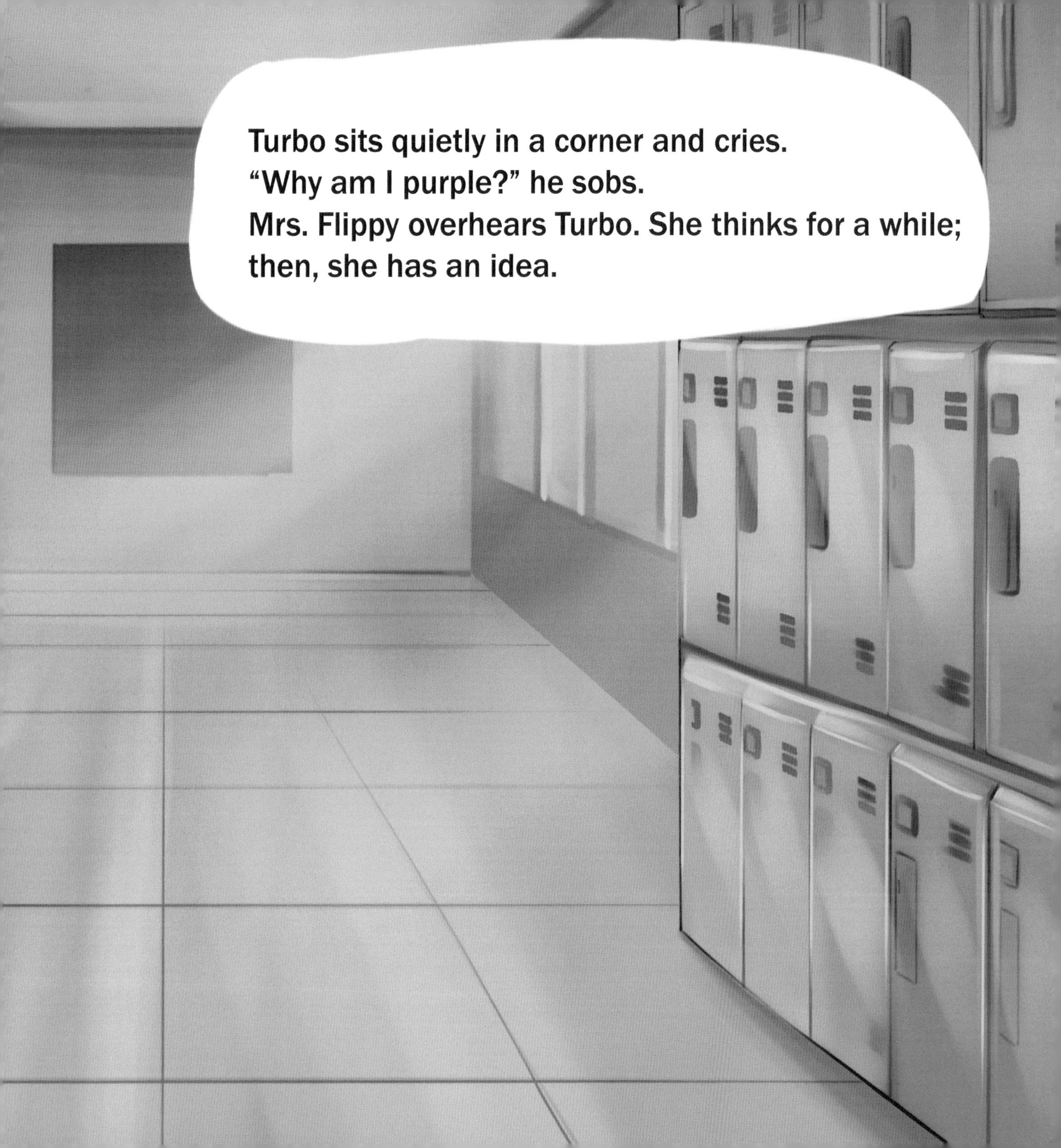
Turbo sits quietly in a corner and cries.
“Why am I purple?” he sobs.
Mrs. Flippy overhears Turbo. She thinks for a while; then, she has an idea.

After recess, Mrs. Flippy says, “Class, I want to teach you the meaning of each color.” “Many of us are green, but does anyone know what the color green means?” Mrs. Flippy asks.
No one answers.

Mrs. Flippy says, “The color green represents growth, renewal, and is sometimes associated with spring.”
“Oooh,” says the class.
“We also have someone here who is another color?” she says. “Turbo is purple.”

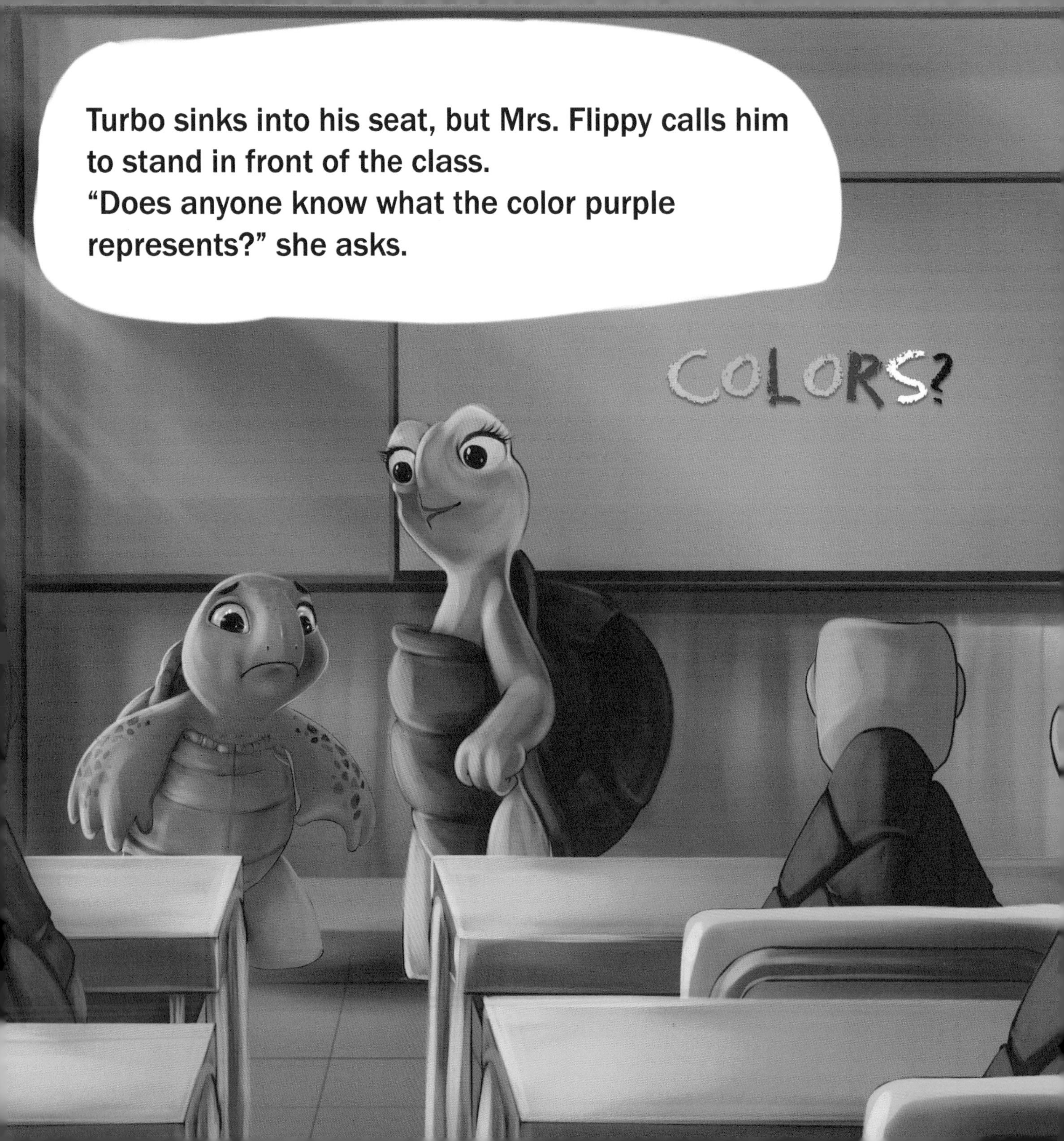

Turbo sinks into his seat, but Mrs. Flippy calls him to stand in front of the class.
"Does anyone know what the color purple represents?" she asks.

"The color purple represents ambition, luxury, and power," says Mrs. Flippy. "It also means greatness, and all things magical."

"I want to be magical," yells a classmate.
"I want to be great," yells another classmate.
Turbo lifts his head and starts to smile.

COLORS?
“You can be anything you want to be,” says Mrs. Flippy. “For today's assignment, choose a paint color and rub it all over yourself. Then come to the front of the class and explain why you chose that color.”

As each student walks up covered in many bright colors,
Turbo realizes he is not the only purple turtle in class
anymore. Mack is purple too!
“I realized Turbo and I are not so different after all,” says
Mack.

"I'm sorry for being rude to you," says Mack. "Can we be friends?"
Turbo nods his head, yes, and they give each other a big hug.

It is time for lunch.
“Sit over here by me, Turbo,” someone shouts.
“There is plenty of room over here,” calls another kid.

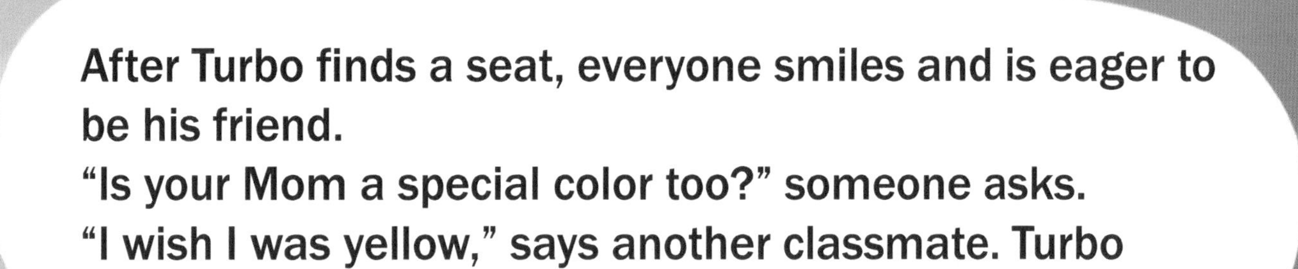

After Turbo finds a seat, everyone smiles and is eager to be his friend.
"Is your Mom a special color too?" someone asks.
"I wish I was yellow," says another classmate. Turbo grins. He makes many friends.

At the end of the day, Mrs. Flippy allows them a few more minutes of recess.

“They play football and hide and seek. Then Mack throws the basketball to Turbo.
Nice catch!

Hard-Shell
Elementary School

The bell rings, and it is time to go home. Turbo sees his mom waiting for him out front.

As Turbo gets in the car, his mom asks, “How was your day?”
Turbo looks up and cracks a smile, “I guess you can say it was colorful!”

They both giggle.
As they drive away, Turbo turns around to take another look at the school. He cannot wait to see his new friends tomorrow.

COLORS?

Printed in Great Britain
by Amazon